For Simon and Chloé

First published in Great Britain in 2003
by Piccadilly Press Ltd.,
5 Castle Road, London NW1 8PR

Text and illustration copyright © Moira Munro, 2003

A catalogue record of this book is available from the British Library

Designed by Fielding Design Ltd
Printed and bound in Belgium by Proost

ISBN:1 85340 772 0 (paperback)
1 85340 767 4 (hardback)

1 3 5 7 9 10 8 6 4 2

Moira Munro lives in Glasgow with her daughter and husband. She has a doctorate
in Ergonomics and was a health and safety specialist for fifteen years.
Reading to her daughter reminded her that there are other pleasures in life, so on her
fortieth birthday she decided to seek new adventures and work as an illustrator.
Visit her website at www.moiramunro.com.

The Bear Who Found His Child

Hamish

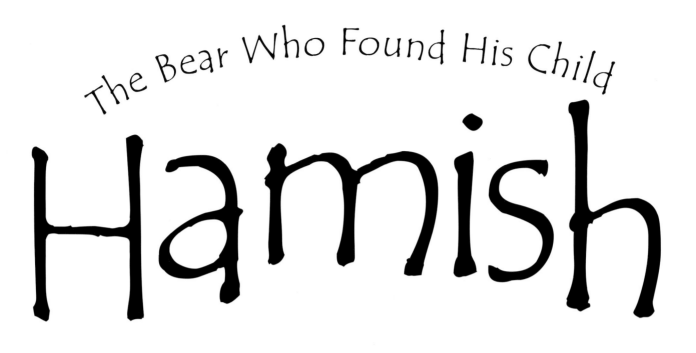

Moira Munro

Piccadilly Press ◆ London

Hamish Bear lived in a
Teddy Bear shop.
It looked like a normal shop,
with teddies arranged
on the shelves.
But really, it was a
magical shop.

When it closed at night,
Hamish and his friends
went through a secret door
into their very own house –
the House of Teddies.

In the House of Teddies, Hamish
had absolutely everything that a
teddy bear could want.

Favourite foods
to feast on . . .

Springy sofas to
party on . . .

Fabulous beds to bounce on . . .

And at the back,
secret play parks
and bright,
sunny gardens.

The House of
Teddies was a truly
magical world.

Hamish was the
liveliest bear in the
House of Teddies.
He liked to be
the first to finish
his porridge.

He liked to have whacking
great pillow fights.

But most of all, Hamish
really liked to ride his
scooter.

And when Big Bear
asked him to do something,
he said, "NO!!!"

(Hamish liked to do
things his own way.)

Inside the shop, all the other bears sat silently and very still – those were the Teddy Bear Rules. They loved to watch the children coming in to choose their teddy bears.

But Hamish always tried to sneak away
to ride his scooter.

In the evenings, Big Bear told the teddies exciting stories about all the bears who had found their own special child to love.

But Hamish thought, "I don't need a special child."

One day in the shop,
Hamish was waiting for a chance
to creep away, when he caught sight
of a little girl. His heart leapt.
She looked like the sweetest girl
he'd ever seen. "Look over here!"
he wanted to shout.
"Please, PLEASE, look at me!"

The little girl slowly turned
round, her eyes searching.
Closer and closer she came.
But just as she was about to see him . . .
she gave up with a sigh.
"Oh no!" thought Hamish. "Don't go away!"
But the little girl wandered out of the shop,
disappointed.

That evening, Hamish didn't want to eat. He didn't want to play. He didn't want to ride his scooter. "How can I get my special child to choose me?" he asked Big Bear. Big Bear thought for a moment. "It *will* happen, Hamish, just like magic. Maybe that girl wasn't your special child. You'll just have to wait and see."

The little girl didn't come in the next day . . .

. . . or the next . . .

. . . or the day after that.

Hamish spent all
his time in the shop,
waiting for her.

And he didn't ride
his scooter once.

He was so sad that Big Bear sat
next to him in the shop.
"Hamish, it looks like she wasn't
your special child after all."
But just then Hamish looked up,
and broke into a huge smile.
"Hurray! She's back!"

This time, Hamish could not stay still. He broke all the Teddy Bear Rules, and scrambled as fast as he could onto a huge pile of books.

She HAD to see him there!

Hamish stood on top of the pile.
His heart was beating ever so fast.
But oh dear!
The little girl was walking
away towards the door!

And then . . .

CRASH! The pile of books came

T U M B L I N G   DOWN!

Hamish flew through the air and landed
right next to the little girl's feet.

"Oh, look at this darling little bear!" cried the girl as she picked him up and fluffed up his fur. "He's just what I've been looking for."

Hamish smiled the biggest, warmest, happiest smile of his life.

And so, Hamish went to live with his special little girl. Some days he felt he could fly.

From time to time, while she was sleeping, he went back to play in the House of Teddies (though he always returned in time for breakfast).

But what Hamish loved best of all was to be with his own special little girl.